Old and New

CONTENTS

NATIONAL GEOGRAPHIC
School Publishing
Hampton-Brown

Words with air, ear, are

Look at each picture. Read the words.

air
_ear
_are

Example:

pear

bear

hair

chair

square

hare

High Frequency Words
began
brother
enough
even
learn
second

Key Words

Look at the pictures.
Read the sentences.

1. Kim always wanted to **learn** to fly a plane.
2. When he got older, his big **brother** **began** to teach him.
3. After **enough** time in the air, he could fly.
4. Now Kim can **even** fly big jets that go over 9 miles in one **second**!

What do you want to learn?

Phonics Games
NGReach.com

Airplane!

by Ann Carey

An airplane is one kind of aircraft. A pilot flies it. An airplane has wings and an engine.

Look at these aircraft.

Which one is an airplane?

Airplanes come in different sizes. Some have one pair of wings. Airplanes can even have three pairs of wings! How many pairs of wings does each of these airplanes have?

Wright brothers

The Wright brothers were the first to fly an airplane. They made an airplane in 1903. The first flight lasted 12 seconds. It was a short flight, but it was long enough. The Wright brothers had flown!

Bessie Coleman

Airplanes were rare at first. Soon more people began to fly airplanes. People went to flying schools to learn how to fly.

In time, people started airlines. Passengers paid a fare to fly in an airplane. Flying was the fastest way to go places!

Airplanes carried mail, too. The U.S. began its first airmail route in 1918. Airmail routes went from coast to coast. Trains also took mail from coast to coast, but airplanes were faster!

A pilot's clothes have changed over time. Today's pilot wears different kinds of clothes from the pilot in the 1920s.

The Wright brothers had to lie down to fly their first airplane!

Today pilots can sit on a chair in the cockpit to fly an airplane. Would you dare to fly a plane? ❖

Airplane Timeline

- 1903 — Wright brother's first flight
- 1910 — First airplane takes off from ship
- 1918 — First airmail flights
- 1919 — First passenger airplanes
- 1927 — First nonstop flight over Atlantic Ocean
- 1937 — First jet engine made
- 1951 — First passenger jet
- 1961 — First space flights

Words with air, ear, are

Read these words.

hair	bear	airplanes	chairs	windows
fare	stairs	meals	men	airport

Find the words with **air**, **ear**, **are**. Use letters to build them.

h a i r

Talk Together

I see chairs at the airport.

Choose words from the box above to complete the sentences.

_eer
ear

Words with eer, ear

Look at each picture. Read the words.

Example:

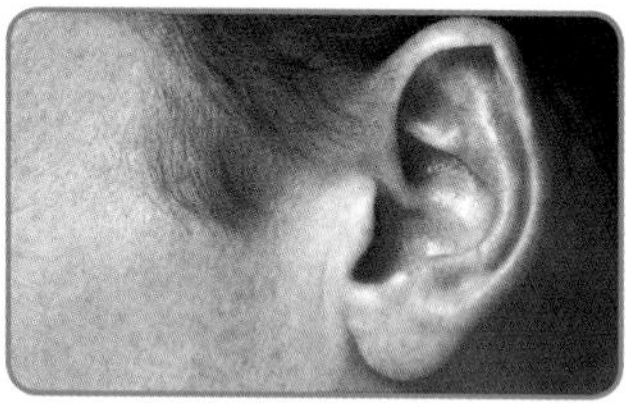

ear

deer

tear

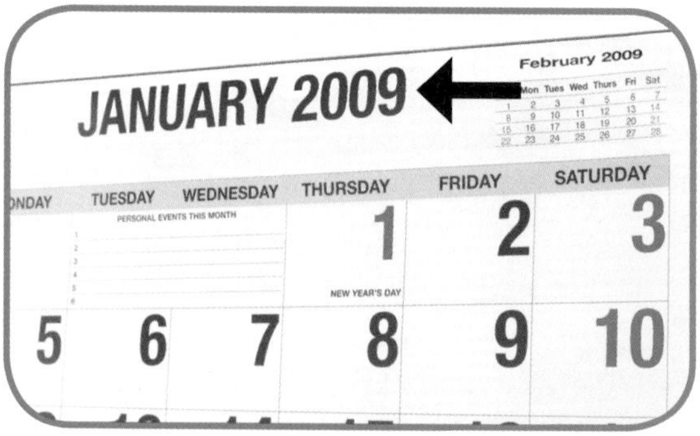

year

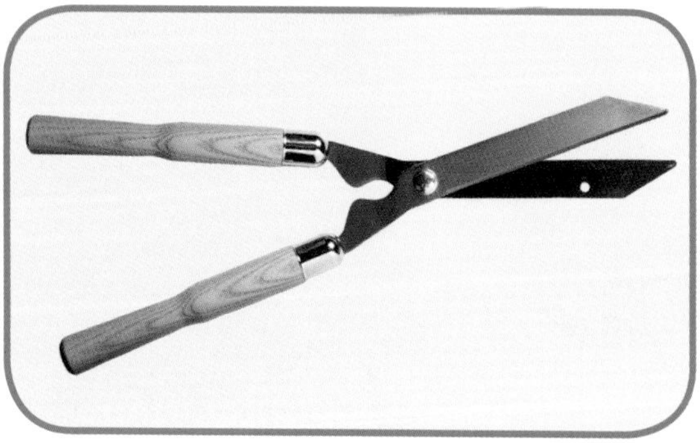

shears

steering wheel

High Frequency Words

- began
- brother
- enough
- even
- learn
- second

Key Words

Look at the picture.
Read the sentences.

Learning From Old Photos

1. You can **learn** a lot, **even** from a photo.
2. My **brother** and I looked at this photo for a few **seconds**!
3. That was **enough** time to see what we had to do.
4. We **began** to use Gran's old butter churn.

Mrs. Grace Herr churns butter on her farm in New York, 1944.

A churn is an old tool.
What old tools can you learn how to use?

Phonics Games
NGReach.com

Each Year at the Farm

by Sterling Spear
illustrated by Judy Love

Each year, my brother and I stay with Gran at her farm. We like to learn how the tools in the barn are used.

My brother peers at a big tool.

"What is this tool?" asks my brother.

"That is a plow," explains Gran.

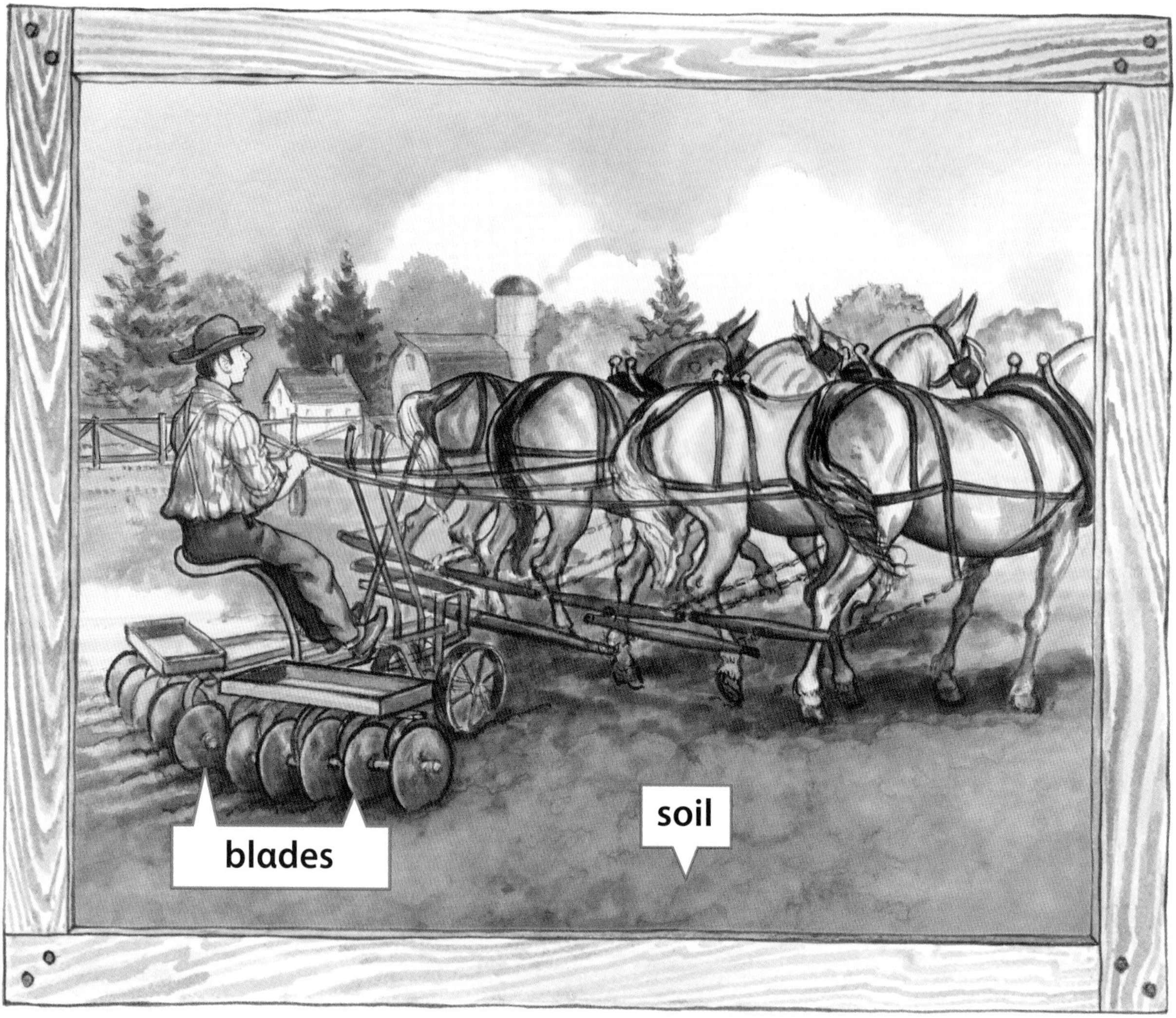

"Horses pulled that plow in the old days," explains Gran. "My dad sat on the seat. The blades of the plow turned the soil over. Then we would plant."

Gran went on. “Today I use a tractor. I hitch a plow to the rear of the tractor. I use the steering wheel to steer. A tractor is faster than horses.”

"What is this tool?" I ask.

"Those are shears for cutting wool off sheep," she tells me. "I used those shears when I began shearing sheep."

"Now I use these new clippers," Gran tells us. "I hear that some people can shear a sheep in less than 100 seconds."

“What is that glass jar?” asks my brother.

I stand near the jar. The glass is clear. I see gears and a crank above the lid.

"That is a butter churn," Gran explains. "We used it to make butter. We put cream in the jar. Next we put the lid on the jar. Then we turned the crank. The cream turned into butter."

We go into the house. Gran smiles. "I made bread today. I even made butter!" She has enough butter for us to smear on the bread.

We like to stay with Gran! ❖

Words with eer, ear

Read these words.

deer	pair	hear	peer	gear
shears	year	near	stare	dare

Find the words with **eer** or **ear**.
Use letters to build them.

d e e r

Talk Together

The girl can peer at the deer.

Choose words from the box above to tell your partner what the girl can do.

At the Airport

Work with a partner. Each of you gets six markers. Player 1 reads a clue and looks in the picture for a match. If you both think a match has been made, Player 1 places a marker on that clue box. Now it is Player 2's turn. Who makes the most matches?

Clue Boxes

A man cannot hear with square earmuffs.

Two brothers peer at airplanes.

People, and even a green deer, go up stairs.

A man began to eat a pear.

An ad says: **A second is not enough to learn to fly.**

A chair with a tear.

Acknowledgments
Grateful acknowledgment is given to the authors, artists, photographers, museums, publishers, and agents for permission to reprint copyrighted material. Every effort has been made to secure the appropriate permission. If any omissions have been made or if corrections are required, please contact the Publisher.

Photographic Credits
CVR (Cover) US Air Force - digital version c/Science Faction/Corbis. **2** (br) PureStock/SuperStock. (cl) Digital Vision/Getty Images. (cr) PhotoDisc/Getty Images. (tl) Stockbyte/Getty Images. (tr) PhotoDisc/Getty Images. **3** (b) Liz Garza Williams/Hampton-Brown/National Geographic School Publishing. **4** Getty Images/Jupiterimages. **5** (b) Jeff Smith/iStockphoto. (bg) PhotoDisc/Getty Images. (c) PhotoDisc/Getty Images. (t) Terry North/iStockphoto. **6** (bg) PhotoDisc/Getty Images. (l) Randy Green/Alamy Images. (r) David Osborn/Alamy Images. (t) sambrogio/iStockphoto. **7** (bg) Museum of Flight/Corbis. (t) Underwood & Underwood/Corbis. **8** (b) Underwood & Underwood/Corbis. (t) Hulton-Deutsch Collection/Corbis. **9** H. Armstrong Roberts/ClassicStock/Corbis. (bg) PhotoDisc/Getty Images. **10** (bg) PhotoDisc/Getty Images. (fg) Museum of Flight/Corbis. (t) Minnesota Historical Society/Corbis. **11** (b) Richard Morrell/Corbis. (t) The Granger Collection, New York. **12** Brooks Kraft/Corbis. **13** (t) Liz Garza Williams/Hampton-Brown/National Geographic School Publishing. **14** (bl) PhotoDisc/Getty Images. (br) laughingmango/iStockphoto. (cl) Dori Oconnell/iStockphoto. (cr) design56/Shutterstock. (tl) PhotoDisc/Getty Images. (tr) Corel. **15** (b) Liz Garza Williams/Hampton-Brown/National Geographic School Publishing. (t) Madeleine Osborne. Series VII.1, Photographs, Box 7.1/3, file "Photographs--Butter churn, 1944," USDA History Collection, Special Collections, National Agricultural Library. **25** (t) Liz Garza Williams/Hampton-Brown/National Geographic School Publishing. **26** (tr) Photodisc/Getty Images.

Illustrator Credits
3, 13 Red Hansen. **16-24** Judy Love. **25-27** Red Hansen

National Geographic School Publishing
Hampton-Brown
www.NGSP.com

Printed in the USA.
Quad Graphics, Leominster, MA

ISBN: 978-0-7362-8049-5

17 18 19
10 9 8 7 6 5

New High Frequency **Words**
began
brother
enough
even
learn
second

Target Sound/Spellings

r-Controlled Vowels **air, ear, are**	**r-Controlled Vowels** **eer, ear**
Selection: **Airplane!**	**Selection:** **Each Year at the Farm**
aircraft	clear
airmail	gears
airplane(s)	hear
chair	near
dare	peer
fair	rear
pair(s)	shearing
rare	shear(s)
wears	smear
	steer
	steering
	year